P9-BZK-224

Clifford
Takes a Trip

Clifford
Takes a Trip

Norman Bridwell

SCHOLASTIC INC.

To Tracy

No part of this publication may be reproduced, stored in a retrieval system, or transmitted in any form or by any means, electronic, mechanical, photocopying, recording, or otherwise, without written permission of the publisher. For information regarding permission, write to Scholastic Inc., Attention: Permissions Department, 557 Broadway, New York, NY 10012.

ISBN 978-1-338-05355-5

Copyright © 1992 by Norman Bridwell. All rights reserved. Published by Scholastic Inc. CLIFFORD and CLIFFORD THE BIG RED DOG are registered trademarks of Norman Bridwell.

Published by Scholastic Inc., *Publishers since 1920*. SCHOLASTIC and associated logos are trademarks and/or registered trademarks of Scholastic Inc.

The publisher does not have any control over and does not assume any responsibility for author or third-party websites or their content.

Printed in China 38

Style: 978-1-338-05355-5
Factory Number: 123386
4/16 - 9/16

This special edition was printed for Kohl's Department Stores, Inc.
(for distribution on behalf of Kohl's Cares, LLC, its wholly owned subsidiary)
by Scholastic Inc.

Hi, I'm Emily Elizabeth.
This is a happy day for me.

This is the last day of school.
Summer vacation is here!
Now I can play with my dog, Clifford.

We don't go on long vacation trips.
It's too hard to get Clifford on a bus
or train.

We only go to places that Clifford can walk to,
like picnics in the park.

Last year was different.

Last year we went to the mountains.

Mommy and Daddy said it was too far

for Clifford to walk.

So we left him with the lady next door.

That night Clifford was so lonely
he began to howl.
He howled and he howled
and he howled —

— until someone threw a shoe at him.
It didn't hurt Clifford's nose,
but it did hurt his feelings.

The next morning Clifford set out to find us.
He sniffed his way along the road.

Clifford didn't mean to make trouble.
But a lot of people had never seen
a big red dog before.

Clifford kept going.
Nothing could stop him.

And then he saw a little old man
trying to fix his truck.
The man needed help.

So Clifford stopped and helped him.
He took the little old man to a garage.

The little old man gave Clifford a little lunch,
to thank him for his help.

Then Clifford set out again.

Nothing stopped him — not even wet cement.

And traffic jams didn't stop him.
Clifford just tiptoed over the cars.
And then . . .

. . . he came to a toll bridge.
Clifford had no money.

But that didn't stop him.

We didn't know Clifford was coming.

I found some new playmates —
two baby bears.
I was having so much fun
I didn't see Mama Bear.

She didn't want strangers
to play with her babies.
She growled.
I was in real trouble.

Then we heard a LOUDER growl.
Guess who was growling!

Mama Bear was surprised.

She even forgot her babies.
I told Clifford that the Mama Bear
was only protecting her children.

Good old Clifford
took the baby bears
back to Mama Bear.

Then he took us all back to camp.
Mommy and Daddy were surprised
to see Clifford.

I told them how Clifford saved my life.